Teddy Bears
Nursery Rhymes

Illustrated by Ann and Mike Ricketts

Brimax · Newmarket · England

Jack and Jill

Jack and Jill went up the hill
To fetch a pail of water;
Jack fell down and broke his crown,
And Jill came tumbling after.

Up Jack got and home did trot,
As fast as he could caper,
He went to bed, to mend his head
With vinegar and brown paper.

Mary, Mary, Quite Contrary

Mary, Mary, quite contrary,
How does your garden grow?
With silver bells and cockle shells,
And pretty maids all in a row.

Ring-a-Ring o'Roses

Ring-a-ring o'roses
A pocket full of posies,
A-tishoo! A-tishoo!
We all fall down.

Baa, Baa, Black Sheep

Baa, baa, black sheep,
Have you any wool?
Yes sir, yes sir,
Three bags full;
One for the master,
And one for the dame,
And one for the little boy
Who lives down the lane.

Wee Willie Winkie

Wee Willie Winkie runs through the town,
Upstairs and downstairs in his night-gown,
Rapping at the window, crying through the lock,
Are the children all in bed, for now it's eight o'clock?

Old King Cole

Old King Cole
Was a merry old soul,
And a merry old soul was he;
He called for his pipe,
And he called for his bowl,
And he called for his fiddlers three.

Every fiddler, he had a fiddle,
And a very fine fiddle had he;
Twee tweedle dee, tweedle dee, went the fiddlers.
Oh, there's none so rare
As can compare
With King Cole and his fiddlers three.

Diddle, Diddle, Dumpling

Diddle, diddle, dumpling, my son John,
Went to bed with his trousers on;
One shoe off and one shoe on,
Diddle, diddle, dumpling, my son John.

Pat-a-Cake, Pat-a-Cake

Pat-a-cake, pat-a-cake, baker's man,
Bake me a cake as fast as you can;
Pat it and prick it, and mark it with B,
Put it in the oven for baby and me.

Mary had a Little Lamb

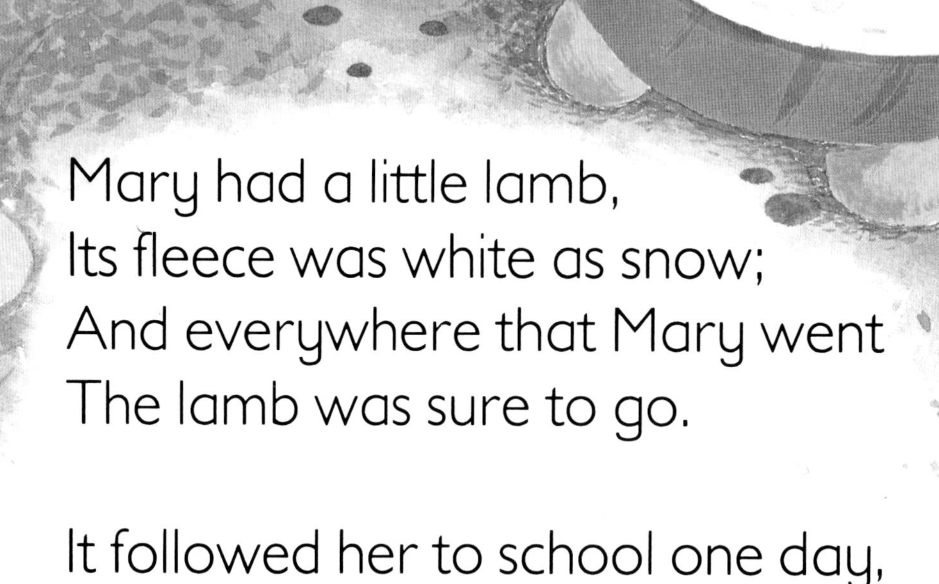

Mary had a little lamb,
Its fleece was white as snow;
And everywhere that Mary went
The lamb was sure to go.

It followed her to school one day,
That was against the rule;
It made the children laugh and play
To see a lamb at school.

And so the teacher turned it out,
But still it lingered near,
And waited patiently about
'Til Mary did appear.

Why does the lamb love Mary so?
The eager children cry;
Why Mary loves the lamb, you know,
The teacher did reply.

Little Jack Horner

Little Jack Horner
Sat in the corner,
Eating a Christmas pie;
He put in his thumb,
And pulled out a plum,
And said, "What a good boy am I!"

Little Miss Muffet

Little Miss Muffet
Sat on a tuffet,
Eating her curds and whey;
There came a big spider,
Who sat down beside her
And frightened Miss Muffet away.

One, Two, Buckle my Shoe

One, two,
Buckle my shoe;
Three, four,
Knock at the door;
Five, six,
Pick up sticks;
Seven, eight,
Lay them straight;
Nine, ten,
A big fat hen;

Eleven, twelve,
Dig and delve;
Thirteen, fourteen,
Maids a-courting;
Fifteen, sixteen,
Maids in the kitchen;
Seventeen, eighteen,
Maids in waiting;
Nineteen, twenty,
My plate's empty.

Little Tommy Tucker

Little Tommy Tucker,
Sings for his supper:
What shall we give him?
White bread and butter.
How shall he cut it
Without a knife?
How will he be married
Without a wife?

See-Saw, Margery Daw

See-saw, Margery Daw,
Jacky shall have a new master;
Jacky shall have but a penny a day,
Because he can't work any faster.

Sing a Song of Sixpence

Sing a song of sixpence,
A pocket full of rye;
Four and twenty blackbirds,
Baked in a pie.

When the pie was opened,
The birds began to sing;
Was not that a dainty dish,
To set before the king?

The king was in his counting house,
Counting out his money;
The queen was in the parlour,
Eating bread and honey.

The maid was in the garden,
Hanging out the clothes,
There came a little blackbird,
And snapped off her nose.

Ride a Cock-Horse

Ride a cock-horse to Banbury Cross,
To see a fine lady upon a white horse;
Rings on her fingers and bells on her toes,
And she shall have music wherever she goes.

Little Boy Blue

Little Boy Blue,
Come blow your horn,
The sheep's in the meadow,
The cow's in the corn;
But where is the boy
Who looks after the sheep?
He's under a haystack,
Fast asleep.
Will you wake him?
No, not I,
For if I do,
He's sure to cry.

Little Bo-Peep

Little Bo-peep has lost her sheep,
And can't tell where to find them;
Leave them alone, and they'll come home,
And bring their tails behind them.

Then up she took her little crook,
Determined for to find them;
She found them indeed, but it made her heart bleed,
For they'd left their tails behind them.

Jack be Nimble

Jack be nimble,
Jack be quick,
Jack jump over
The candle stick.

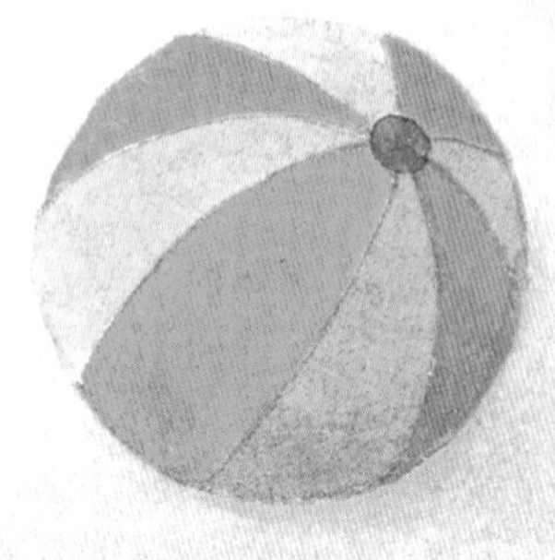

Twinkle, Twinkle, Little Star

Twinkle, twinkle, little star,
How I wonder what you are!
Up above the world so high,
Like a diamond in the sky.

When the blazing sun is gone,
When he nothing shines upon,
Then you show your little light,
Twinkle, twinkle, all the night.